For Dylan, with all my love x
~T C

For Karyn Anderton
~T M

LITTLE TIGER PRESS
An imprint of Magi Publications
1 The Coda Centre, 189 Munster Road,
London SW6 6AW
www.littletigerpress.com

First published in Great Britain 2011

A CIP catalogue record for this book is available from the British Library

All rights reserved • ISBN 978-1-84895-136-5

Printed in China

LTP/1800/0138/1010

2 4 6 8 10 9 7 5 3 1

Oh Dylan!

Tracey Corderoy • Tina Macnaughton

LITTLE TIGER PRESS
London

One breezy day, four little ducklings were making a daisy chain.

"Pick and thread!" chanted Polly, Molly and Holly.

"Look at me!" chuckled Dylan, all tied up in a big flowery knot!

"Now," said Mummy, "we're off to the pond for your very first swim. Hold on to the daisy chain then you won't get lost."

"It's a choo-choo chain!" cried Dylan. "Choo-choo!"

Polly, Molly, Holly and Dylan skipped along behind
Mummy, singing a springtime song . . .

"Four little ducklings all in a row,
Skipping across the bridge we go!
Wiggle our tails – we're on our way
Down to the pond to splash and play!"

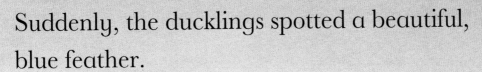

Suddenly, the ducklings spotted a beautiful,
blue feather.

"So pretty!" gasped Polly, Molly and Holly.

"Come back!" cried Dylan as the feather
blew away.

Then he had a *wonderful* idea . . .

On the other side of the bridge, some baby lambs were playing catch-the-petals.

"*We* want to play too!" said Polly.

"All right," smiled Mummy. She counted her ducklings as they hopped off the bridge. "Polly, Molly, Holly and . . .

"OH MY!" she gasped.
"Where's Dylan?"

All in a fluster
and a flap, everyone
searched for Dylan.

Suddenly, Molly spotted him stuck up a tree!
  "Surprise!" cried Dylan. "I got the pretty
feather for you!"

"Oh, *Dylan*," said Mummy. "You *are* a sweetie!
  But what did Mummy say about not getting lost?
Now hold on to the choo-choo chain."
  "And don't let go!" quacked Polly.

On they went into the wood, singing their song . . .

"Four little ducklings all in a row,
Counting the flowers as we go!
Flutter our wings — we're on our way
Down to the pond to dive and play!"

"Mmmm, *lovely!*" cried the girls, sniffing the flowers.
"A-ccchhhoooo!" sneezed Dylan.
Then he had a *wonderful* idea . . .

At the top of a hill, some baby hedgehogs were playing roly-poly!

"*We* want to roll too!" said Polly.

"All right," smiled Mummy. She counted her ducklings as they tumbled down the hill.

"Polly, Molly, Holly and . . .

"WAIT!" she flapped. "Where's Dylan?"

With wings a-flutter and
feathers flying, everyone
searched for Dylan.
Then suddenly a whirlwind of
fluff came spinning towards them . . .

"Surprise!" cried Dylan. "I picked some pretty flowers for you!"

"Oh, *Dylan*," said Mummy. "You *are* kind! But you forgot what Mummy told you *again* . . ."

"Don't let go of the daisy chain!" yelled his sisters.

On they waddled, under a hedge and *at last* they saw . . .

. . . the pond!

"*Phew!*" gasped Mummy.

"All safely here!"

Polly, Molly and Holly dipped their
toes into the water.

"But it's *c-c-cold*!" they shivered.

"We don't like it!"

Then suddenly,

splash!

Dylan was in . . .

. . . and – *wow* – this was *fun*!

"Look!" cried Dylan. "Look at me!"

He splished and splashed and swam
and swam until, all too soon, it was
time to go.

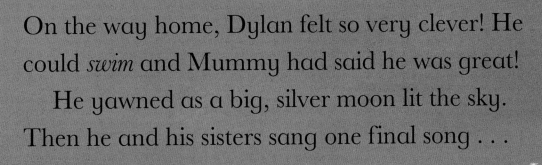

On the way home, Dylan felt so very clever! He
could *swim* and Mummy had said he was great!
He yawned as a big, silver moon lit the sky.
Then he and his sisters sang one final song . . .

"Four sleepy ducklings all in a row,
Waddling back for tea we go.
Tiny stars begin to peep,
Soon we'll all be fast asleep . . . "

When they got home, Mummy toasted muffins for tea. Then she counted her ducklings up to the table.

"Polly, Molly, Holly and . . . Oh *dear*," she sighed. "Not again! *Where's Dylan?*"

Polly wriggled, Molly giggled but Holly
whispered in Mummy's ear. Then they
peeped round the door . . .

. . . and there, curled up in his choo-choo chain, was *Dylan*.
"Night-night," giggled his sisters as he gave a tiny snore.
"Sleep tight," whispered Mummy. "Sweet dreams!"